2R
1.36
Ho

D1160089

More
Jataka Tales

More Jataka Tales

Re-told by
Ellen C. Babbitt

With illustrations by
Ellsworth Young

APPLETON-CENTURY-CROFTS, INC.
NEW YORK

DEDICATED

to

RUDYARD KIPLING

in the name of all children

who troop to his call

FOREWORD

FOREWORD

The continued success of the "Jataka Tales," as retold
and published ten years ago, has led to this second and com-
panion volume. Who that has read or told stories to
children has not been lured on by the subtle flattery of their
cry for "more"?

Dr. Felix Adler, in his Foreword to "Jataka Tales," says
that long ago he was "captivated by the charm of the Jataka
Tales." Little children have not only felt this charm, but
they have discovered that they can read the stories to themselves. And so "More Jataka Tales" were found in the volume translated from the Sanskrit into English by a group
of Cambridge scholars and published by the University
Press.

The Jataka tales, regarded as historic in the Third Cen-
tury B. C., are the oldest collection of folk-lore extant.
They come down to us from that dim for-off time when our
forebears told tales around the same hearthfire on the roof
of the world. Professor Rhys Davids speaks of them as

FOREWORD

"a priceless record of the childhood of our race. The same stories are found in Greek, Latin, Arabic, Persian, and in most European languages. The Greek versions of the Jataka tales were adapted and ascribed to the famous story-teller, Æsop, and under his name handed down as a continual feast for the children in the West,—tales first invented to please and instruct our far-off cousins in the East." Here East, though East, meets West!

A "Guild of Jataka Translators," under Professor E. B. Cowell, professor of Sanskrit in the University of Cambridge, brought out the complete edition of the Jataka between 1895 and 1907. It is from this source that "Jataka Tales" and "More Jataka Tales" have been retold.

Of these stories, spread over Europe through literary channels, Professor Cowell says, "They are the stray waifs of literature, in the course of their long wanderings coming to be recognized under widely different aspects, as when they are used by Boccaccio, or Chaucer, or La Fontaine."

CONTENTS

CONTENTS

More
Jataka Tales

MORE JATAKA TALES

I

THE GIRL MONKEY AND THE STRING OF PEARLS

ONE day the king went for a long walk in the woods. When he came back to his own garden, he sent for his family to come down to the lake for a swim.

When they were all ready to go into the water, the queen and her ladies left their jewels in charge of the servants, and then went down into the lake.

As the queen put her string of pearls away in a box, she was watched by a Girl Monkey who sat in the branches of a tree near-by. This Girl Monkey wanted to get the queen's string of pearls, so she sat still and watched, hoping that the servant in charge of the pearls would go to sleep.

At first the servant kept her eyes on the jewel-box. But by and by she began to nod, and then she fell fast asleep.

As soon as the Monkey saw this, quick as the wind she jumped down, opened the box, picked up the string of pearls, and quick as the wind she was up in the tree again, holding the pearls very carefully. She put the string of pearls on, and then, for fear the guards in the garden would see the pearls, the Monkey hid them in a hole in the tree. Then she sat near-by looking as if nothing had happened.

By and by the servant awoke. She looked in the box, and finding that the string of pearls was not there, she cried, "A man has run off with the queen's string of pearls."

Up ran the guards from every side.

The servant said: "I sat right here beside the box where the queen put her string of pearls. I did not move from the place. But the day is hot, and I was tired. I must have fallen asleep. The pearls were gone when I awoke."

The guards told the king that the pearls were gone.

"Find the man who stole the pearls," said the king. Away went the guards looking high and low for the thief.

After the king had gone, the chief guard said to himself:

"There is something strange here. These pearls," thought he, "were lost in the garden. There was a strong guard at the gates, so that no one from the outside could get into the garden. On the other hand, there are hundreds of

4

Monkeys here in the garden.   Perhaps one of the Girl Monkeys took the string of pearls."

Then the chief guard thought of a trick that would tell whether a Girl Monkey had taken the pearls.   So he bought a number of strings of bright-colored glass beads.

After dark that night the guards hung the strings of glass beads here and there on the low bushes in the garden.   When the Monkeys saw the strings of bright-colored beads the next morning, each Monkey ran for a string.

But the Girl Monkey who had taken the queen's string of pearls did not come down.   She sat near the hole where she had hidden the pearls.

The other Monkeys were greatly pleased with their strings of beads.   They chattered to one another about them.   "It is too bad you did not get one," they said to her as she sat quietly, saying nothing.   At last she could stand it no longer.   She put on the queen's string of pearls and came down, saying proudly: "You have only strings of glass beads.   See my string of pearls!"

Then the chief of the guards, who had been hiding nearby, caught the Girl Monkey.   He took her at once to the king.

"It was this Girl Monkey, your Majesty, who took the pearls."

6

GIRL MONKEY AND STRING OF PEARLS

The king was glad enough to get the pearls, but he asked the chief guard how he had found out who took them.

The chief guard told the king that he knew no one could have come into the garden and so he thought they must have been taken by one of the Monkeys in the garden.   Then he told the king about the trick he had played with the beads.

"You are the right man in the right place," said the king, and he thanked the chief of the guards over and over again.

II

THE THREE FISHES

ONCE upon a time three Fishes lived in a far-away river. They were named Thoughtful, Very-Thoughtful, and Thoughtless.

One day they left the wild country where no men lived, and came down the river to live near a town.

Very-Thoughtful said to the other two: "There is danger all about us here. Fishermen come to the river here to catch fish with all sorts of nets and lines. Let us go back again to the wild country where we used to live."

But the other two Fishes were so lazy and so greedy that they kept putting off their going from day to day.

But one day Thoughtful and Thoughtless went swimming on ahead of Very-Thoughtful and they did not see the fisherman's net and rushed into it. Very-Thoughtful saw them rush into the net.

"I must save them," said Very-Thoughtful.

So swimming around the net, he splashed in the water in

8

front of it, like a Fish that had broken through the net and gone up the river. Then he swam back of the net and

splashed about there like a Fish that had broken through and gone down the river.

9

The fisherman saw the splashing water and thought the Fishes had broken through the net and that one had gone up the river, the other down, so he pulled in the net by one corner. That let the two Fishes out of the net and away they went to find Very-Thoughful.

"You saved our lives, Very-Thoughtful," they said, "and now we are willing to go back to the wild country."

So back they all went to their old home where they lived safely ever after.

III

THE TRICKY WOLF AND THE RATS

ONCE upon a time a Big Rat lived in the forest, and many hundreds of other Rats called him their Chief.

A Tricky Wolf saw this troop of Rats, and began to plan how he could catch them. He wanted to eat them, but how was he to get them? At last he thought of a plan. He went to a corner near the home of the Rats and waited until he saw one of them coming. Then he stood up on his hind legs.

The Chief of the Rats said to the Wolf, "Wolf, why do you stand on your hind legs?"

"Because I am lame," said the Tricky Wolf. "It hurts me to stand on my front legs."

"And why do you keep your mouth open?" asked the Rat.

"I keep my mouth open so that I may drink in all the air I can," said the Wolf. "I live on air; it is my only food day after day. I can not run or walk, so I stay here. I

try not to complain." When the Rats went away the Wolf lay down.

The Chief of the Rats was sorry for the Wolf, and he went each night and morning with all the other Rats to talk with the Wolf, who seemed so poor, and who did not complain.

Each time as the Rats were leaving, the Wolf caught and ate the last one. Then he wiped his lips, and looked as if nothing had happened.

Each night there were fewer Rats at bedtime. Then they asked the Chief of the Rats what the trouble was. He could not be sure, but he thought the Wolf was to blame.

So the next day the Chief said to the other Rats, "You go first this time and I will go last."

They did so, and as the Chief of the Rats went by, the

Wolf made a spring at him. But the Wolf was not quick enough, and the Chief of the Rats got away.

"So this is the food you eat. Your legs are not so lame as they were. You have played your last trick, Wolf," said the Chief of the Rats, springing at the Wolf's throat. He bit the Wolf, so that he died.

And ever after the Rats lived happily in peace and quiet.

IV

THE WOODPECKER, TURTLE, AND DEER

ONCE upon a time a Deer lived in a forest near a lake. Not far from the same lake, a Woodpecker had a nest in the top of a tree; and in the lake lived a Turtle. The three were friends, and lived together happily.

A hunter, wandering about in the wood, saw the footprints of the Deer near the edge of the lake. "I must trap the Deer, going down into the water," he said, and setting a strong trap of leather, he went his way.

Early that night when the Deer went down to drink, he was caught in the trap, and he cried the cry of capture.

At once the Woodpecker flew down from her tree-top, and the Turtle came out of the water to see what could be done.

Said the Woodpecker to the Turtle: "Friend, you have teeth; you gnaw through the leather trap. I will go and see to it that the hunter keeps away. If we both do our best our friend will not lose his life."

So the Turtle began to gnaw the leather, and the Woodpecker flew to the hunter's house.

At dawn the hunter came, knife in hand, to the front door

of his house.

The Woodpecker, flapping her wings, flew at the hunter and struck him in the face.

The hunter turned back into the house and lay down for a little while. Then he rose up again, and took his knife. He said to himself: "When I went out by the front door, a Bird flew in my face; now I will go out by the back door." So he did.

The Woodpecker thought: "The hunter went out by the front door before, so now he will leave by the back door." So the Woodpecker sat in a tree near the back door.

When the hunter came out the bird flew at him again, flapping her wings in the hunter's face.

Then the hunter turned back and lay down again. When the sun arose, he took his knife, and started out once more.

This time the Woodpecker flew back as fast as she could fly to her friends, crying, "Here comes the hunter!"

By this time the Turtle had gnawed through all the pieces of the trap but one. The leather was so hard that it made his teeth feel as if they would fall out. His mouth was all covered with blood. The Deer heard the Woodpecker, and saw the hunter, knife in hand, coming on. With a strong pull the Deer broke this last piece of the trap, and ran into the woods.

The Woodpecker flew up to her nest in the tree-top.

But the Turtle was so weak he could not get away. He

lay where he was. The hunter picked him up and threw him into a bag, tying it to a tree.

The Deer saw that the Turtle was taken, and made up his mind to save his friend's life. So the Deer let the hunter see him.

The hunter seized his knife and started after the Deer. The Deer, keeping just out of his reach, led the hunter into the forest.

When the Deer saw that they had gone far into the forest he slipped away from the hunter, and swift as the wind, he went by another way to where he had left the Turtle.

But the Turtle was not there. The Deer called, "Turtle, Turtle!"; and the Turtle called out, "Here I am in a bag hanging on this tree."

Then the Deer lifted the bag with his horns, and throwing it upon the ground, he tore the bag open, and let the Turtle out.

The Woodpecker flew down from her nest, and the Deer said to them: "You two friends saved my life, but if we stay here talking, the hunter will find us, and we may not get away. So do you, Friend Woodpecker, fly away. And you, Friend Turtle, dive into the water. I will hide in the forest."

The hunter did come back, but neither the Deer, nor the Turtle, nor the Woodpecker was to be seen. He found his torn bag, and picking that up he went back to his home.

The three friends lived together all the rest of their lives.

V

THE GOLDEN GOOSE

ONCE upon a time there was a Goose who had beautiful golden feathers. Not far away from this Goose lived a poor, a very poor woman, who had two daughters. The Goose saw that they had a hard time to get along and said he to himself:

"If I give them one after another of my golden feathers, the mother can sell them, and with the money they bring she and her daughters can then live in comfort."

So away the Goose flew to the poor woman's house.

Seeing the Goose, the woman said: "Why do you come here? We have nothing to give you."

"But I have something to give you," said the Goose. "I will give my feathers, one by one, and you can sell them for enough so that you and your daughters can live in comfort."

So saying the Goose gave her one of his feathers, and then flew away. From time to time he came back, each time leaving another feather.

The mother and her daughters sold the beautiful feathers for enough money to keep them in comfort. But one day the mother said to her daughters: "Let us not trust this Goose. Some day he may fly away and never come back.

Then we should be poor again. Let us get all of his feathers the very next time he comes."

The daughters said: "This will hurt the Goose. We will not do such a thing."

But the mother was greedy. The next time the Golden

Goose came she took hold of him with both hands, and pulled out every one of his feathers.

Now the Golden Goose has strange feathers. If his feathers are plucked out against his wish, they no longer re-

main golden but turn white and are of no more value than chicken-feathers. The new ones that come in are not golden, but plain white.

As time went on his feathers grew again, and then he flew away to his home and never came back again.

VI

THE STUPID MONKEYS

ONCE upon a time a king gave a holiday to all the
people in one of his cities.

The king's gardener thought to himself: "All
my friends are having a holiday in the city. I could go into the city and enjoy myself with them if I did not have to
water the trees here in this garden. I know what I will do.
I will get the Monkeys to water the young trees for me."
In those days, a tribe of Monkeys lived in the king's garden.

So the gardener went to the Chief of the Monkeys, and
said: "You are lucky Monkeys to be living in the king's garden. You have a fine place to play in. You have the best
of food—nuts, fruit, and the young shoots of trees to eat.
You have no work at all to do. You can play all day, every
day. To-day my friends are having a holiday in the city,
and I want to enjoy myself with them. Will you water the
young trees so that I can go away?"

"Oh, yes!" said the Chief of the Monkeys. "We shall be
glad to do that."

24

THE STUPID MONKEYS

"Do not forget to water the trees when the sun goes down. See they have plenty of water, but not too much," said the gardener. Then he showed them where the watering-pots were kept, and went away.

When the sun went down the Monkeys took the watering-pots, and began to water the young trees. "See that each tree has enough water," said the Chief of the Monkeys.

"How shall we know when each tree has enough?" they asked. The Chief of the Monkeys had no good answer, so

25

he said: "Pull up each young tree and look at the length of its roots. Give a great deal of water to those with long roots, but only a little to those trees that have short roots."

Then those stupid Monkeys pulled up all the young trees to see which trees had long roots and which had short roots.

When the gardener came back the next day, the poor young trees were all dead.

VII

THE CUNNING WOLF

O NCE upon a time the people in a certain town went
out into the woods for a holiday. They took
baskets full of good things to eat. But when
noontime came they ate all the meat they had brought with
them, not leaving any for supper.

"I will get some fresh meat. We will make a fire here
and roast it," said one of the men.

So taking a club, he went to the lake where the animals
came to drink. He lay down, club in hand, pretending to be
dead.

When the animals came down to the lake they saw the
man lying there and they watched him for some time.

"That man is playing a trick on us, I believe," said the
King of the Wolves. "The rest of you stay here while I
will see whether he is really dead, or whether he is pretending to be dead."

27

Then the cunning King of the Wolves crept up to the man and slyly pulled at his club.

At once the man pulled back on his club.

Then the King of the Wolves ran off saying: "If you had been dead, you would not have pulled back on your club when I tried to pull it away. I see your trick. You pre-

tend you are dead so that you may kill one of us for your supper."

The man jumped up and threw his club at the King of the Wolves. But he missed his aim. He looked for the other animals but there was not one in sight. They had all run away.

28

THE CUNNING WOLF

Then the man went back to his friends, saying: "I tried to get fresh meat by playing a trick on the animals, but the cunning Wolf played a better trick on me, and I could not get one of them."

THE PENNY-WISE MONKEY

VIII

THE PENNY-WISE MONKEY

ONCE upon a time the king of a large and rich country gathered together his army to take a far-away little country.

The king and his soldiers marched all morning long and then went into camp in the forest.

When they fed the horses they gave them some peas to eat. One of the Monkeys living in the forest saw the peas and jumped down to get some of them. He filled his mouth and hands with them, and up into the tree he went again, and sat down to eat the peas.

As he sat there eating the peas, one pea fell from his hand to the ground. At once the greedy Monkey dropped all the peas he had in his hands, and ran down to hunt for the lost pea. But he could not find that one pea. He climbed up into his tree again, and sat still looking very glum. "To get more, I threw away what I had," he said to himself.

The king had watched the Monkey, and he said to him·

self: "I will not be like this foolish Monkey, who lost much to gain a little. I will go back to my own country and enjoy what I now have."

So he and his men marched back home.

IX

THE RED-BUD TREE

ONCE upon a time four young princes heard a story about a certain wonderful tree, called the Red-Bud Tree. No one of them had ever seen a Red-Bud Tree, and each prince wished to be the first to see one.

So the eldest prince asked the driver of the king's chariot to take him deep into the woods where this tree grew. It was still very early in the spring and the tree had no leaves, nor buds. It was black and bare like a dead tree. The prince could not understand why this was called a Red-Bud Tree, but he asked no questions.

Later in the spring, the next son went with the driver of the king's chariot to see the Red-Bud Tree. At this time it was covered with red buds.

The tree was all covered with green leaves when the third son went into the woods a little later to see it. He asked no questions about it, but he could see no reason for calling it the Red-Bud Tree.

Some time after this the youngest prince begged to be

taken to see the Red-Bud Tree. By this time it was covered with little bean-pods.

When he came back from the woods he ran into the garden where his brothers were playing, crying, "I have seen the Red-Bud Tree."

"So have I," said the eldest prince. "It did not look like much of a tree to me," said he; "it looked like a dead tree. It was black and bare."

"What makes you say that?" said the second son. "The tree has hundreds of beautiful red buds. This is why it is called the Red-Bud Tree."

34

THE RED-BUD TREE

The third prince said: "Red buds, did you say? Why do you say it has red buds? It is covered with green leaves."

The prince who had seen the tree last laughed at his brothers, saying: "I have just seen that tree, and it is not like a dead tree. It has neither red buds nor green leaves on it. It is covered with little bean-pods."

The king heard them and waited until they stopped talking. Then he said: "My sons, you have all four seen the same tree, but each of you saw it at a different time of the year."

X

THE WOODPECKER AND THE LION

ONE day while a Lion was eating his dinner a bone stuck in his throat. It hurt so that he could not finish his dinner. He walked up and down, up and down, roaring with pain.

A Woodpecker lit on a branch of a tree near-by, and hearing the Lion, she said, "Friend, what ails you?" The Lion told the Woodpecker what the matter was, and the Woodpecker said: "I would take the bone out of your throat, friend, but I do not dare to put my head into your mouth, for fear I might never get it out again. I am afraid you might eat me."

"O Woodpecker, do not be afraid," the Lion said. "I will not eat you. Save my life if you can!"

"I will see what I can do for you," said the Woodpecker. "Open your mouth wide." The Lion did as he was told, but the Woodpecker said to himself: "Who knows what this Lion will do? I think I will be careful."

THE WOODPECKER AND THE LION

So the Woodpecker put a stick between the Lion's upper and lower jaws so that he could not shut his mouth.

Then the Woodpecker hopped into the Lion's mouth and hit the end of the bone with his beak. The second time he hit it, the bone fell out.

The Woodpecker hopped out of the Lion's mouth, and hit the stick so that it too fell out. Then the Lion could shut his mouth.

At once the Lion felt very much better, but not one word of thanks did he say to the Woodpecker.

One day later in the summer, the Woodpecker said to the Lion, "I want you to do something for me."

"Do something for you?" said the Lion. "You mean you want me to do something more for you. I have already done a great deal for you. You cannot expect me to do anything more for you. Do not forget that once I had you in my mouth, and I let you go. That is all that you can ever expect me to do for you."

The Woodpecker said no more, but he kept away from the Lion from that day on.

XI

THE OTTERS AND THE WOLF

ONE day a Wolf said to her mate, "A longing has come upon me to eat fresh fish."

"I will go and get some for you," said he and he went down to the river.

There he saw two Otters standing on the bank looking for fish. Soon one of the Otters saw a great fish, and entering the water with a bound, he caught hold of the tail of the fish.

But the fish was strong and swam away, dragging the Otter after him. "Come and help me," the Otter called back to his friend. "This great fish will be enough for both of us!"

So the other Otter went into the water. The two together were able to bring the fish to land. "Let us divide the fish into two parts."

"I want the half with the head on," said one.

"You cannot have that half. That is mine," said the other. "You take the tail."

The Wolf heard the Otters and he went up to them.

Seeing the Wolf, the Otters said: "Lord of the gray-grass color, this fish was caught by both of us together. We cannot agree about dividing him. Will you divide him for us?"

The Wolf cut off the tail and gave it to one, giving the head to the other. He took the large middle part for him-

self, saying to them, "You can eat the head and the tail without quarreling." And away he ran with the body of the fish. The Otters stood and looked at each other. They had nothing to say, but each thought to himself that the Wolf had run off with the best of the fish.

THE OTTERS AND THE WOLF

The Wolf was pleased and said to himself, as he ran toward home, "Now I have fresh fish for my mate."

His mate, seeing him coming, came to meet him, saying: "How did you get fish? You live on land, not in the water."

Then he told her of the quarrel of the Otters. "I took the fish as pay for settling their quarrel," said he.

XII

HOW THE MONKEY SAVED HIS TROOP

A MANGO-TREE grew on the bank of a great river. The fruit fell from some of the branches of this tree into the river, and from other branches it fell on the ground.

Every night a troop of Monkeys gathered the fruit that lay on the ground and climbed up into the tree to get the mangoes, which were like large, juicy peaches.

One day the king of the country stood on the bank of this same river, but many miles below where the mango-tree grew. The king was watching the fishermen with their nets.

As they drew in their nets, the fishermen found not only fishes but a strange fruit. They went to the king with the strange fruit. "What is this?" asked the king.

"We do not know, O King," they said.

"Call the foresters," said the king, "They will know what it is."

So they called the foresters and they said that it was a mango.

"Is it good to eat?" asked the king.

The foresters said it was very good.   So the king cut the

mango and giving some to the princes, he ate some of it himself.   He liked it very much, and they all liked it.

Then the king said to the foresters, "Where does the mango-tree grow?"

The foresters told him that it grew on the river bank many miles farther up the river.

"Let us go and see the tree and get some mangoes," said the king.

So he had many rafts joined together, and they went up the river until they came to the place where the mango-tree grew.

The foresters said, "O King, this is the mango-tree."

"We will land here," said the king, and they did so. The king and all the men with him gathered the mangoes that lay on the ground under the tree. They all liked them so well that the king said, "Let us stay here to-night, and gather more fruit in the morning." So they had their supper under the trees, and then lay down to sleep.

When all was quiet, the Chief of the Monkeys came with his troop. All the mangoes on the ground had been eaten, so the monkeys jumped from branch to branch, picking and eating mangoes, and chattering to one another. They made so much noise that they woke up the king. He called his archers saying: "Stand under the mango-tree and shoot the Monkeys as they come down to the ground to get away. Then in the morning we shall have Monkey's flesh as well as mangoes to eat."

The Monkeys saw the archers standing around with their

45

arrows ready to shoot. Fearing death, the Monkeys ran to their Chief, saying: "O Chief, the archers stand around the tree ready to shoot us! What shall we do?" They shook with fear.

The Chief said: "Do not fear; I will save you. Stay where you are until I call you."

The Monkeys were comforted, for he had always helped them whenever they had needed help.

Then the Chief of the Monkeys ran out on the branch of the mango-tree that hung out over the river. The long branches of the tree across the river did not quite meet the branch he stood on. The Chief said to himself: "If the Monkeys try to jump across from this tree to that, some of them will fall into the water and drown. I must save them, but how am I to do it? I know what I shall do. I shall make a bridge of my back."

So the Chief reached across and took hold of the longest branch of the tree across the river. He called, "Come, Monkeys; run out on this branch, step on my back, and then run along the branch of the other tree."

The Monkeys did as the Chief told them to do. They ran along the branch, stepped on his back, then ran along the branch of the other tree. They swung themselves down to the ground, and away they went back to their home.

HOW THE MONKEY SAVED HIS TROOP

The king saw all that was done by the Chief and his troop. "That big Monkey," said the king to the archers, "saved the whole troop. I will see to it that he is taken care of the rest of his life."

And the king kept his promise.

XIII

THE HAWKS AND THEIR FRIENDS

A FAMILY of Hawks lived on an island in a lake not far from the great forest. On the northern shore of this lake lived a Lion, King of Beasts. On the eastern shore lived a Kingfisher. On the southern shore of the lake lived a Turtle.

"Have you many friends near here?" the Mother Hawk asked the Father Hawk.

"No, not one in this part of the forest," he said.

"You must find some friends. We must have some one who can help us if ever we are in danger, or in trouble," said the Mother Hawk.

"With whom shall I make friends?" asked the Father Hawk.

"With the Kingfisher, who lives on the eastern shore, and with the Lion on the north," said the Mother Hawk, "and with the Turtle who lives on the southern shore of this lake."

The Father Hawk did so.

THE HAWKS AND THEIR FRIENDS

One day men hunted in the great forest from morning until night, but found nothing. Not wishing to go home empty-handed, they went to the island to see what they could find there.

"Let us stay here to-night," they said, "and see what we can find in the morning."

So they made beds of leaves for themselves and lay down to sleep. They had made their beds under the tree in which the Hawks had their nest.

But the hunters could not go to sleep because they were bothered by the flies and mosquitoes. At last the hunters got up and made a fire on the shore of the lake, so that the smoke would drive away the flies and mosquitoes. The smoke awoke the birds, and the young ones cried out.

"Did you hear that?" said one of the hunters. "That was the cry of birds! They will do very well for our breakfast. There are young ones in that nest." And the hunters put more wood on the fire, and made it blaze up.

Then the Mother bird said to the Father: "These men are planning to eat our young ones. We must ask our friends to save us. Go to the Kingfisher and tell him what danger we are in."

The Father Hawk flew with all speed to the Kingfisher's nest and woke him with his cry.

"Why have you come?" asked the Kingfisher.

Then the Father Hawk told the Kingfisher what the hunters planned to do.

"Fear not," said the Kingfisher. "I will help you. Go back quickly and comfort my friend your mate, and say that I am coming."

So the Father Hawk flew back to his nest, and the Kingfisher flew to the island and went into the lake near the place where the fire was burning.

While the Father Hawk was away, one of the hunters had climbed up into the tree. Just as he neared the nest, the Kingfisher, beating the water with his wings, sprinkled water on the fire and put it out.

Down came the hunter to make another fire. When it was burning well he climbed the tree again. Once more the Kingfisher put it out. As often as a fire was made, the Kingfisher put it out. Midnight came and the Kingfisher was now very tired.

The Mother Hawk noticed this and said to her mate: "The Kingfisher is tired out. Go and ask the Turtle to help us so that the Kingfisher may have a rest."

The Father Hawk flew down and said, "Rest awhile, Friend Kingfisher; I will go and get the Turtle."

So the Father Hawk flew to the southern shore and wakened the Turtle.

"What is your errand, Friend?" asked the Turtle.

"Danger has come to us," said the Father Hawk, and he told the Turtle about the hunters. "The Kingfisher has been working for hours, and now he is very tired. That is why I have come to you."

The Turtle said, "I will help you at once."

Then the Turtle went to the island where the Hawks lived. He dived into the water, collected some mud, and put out the fire with it. Then he lay still.

The hunters cried: "Why should we bother to get the young Hawks? Let us kill this Turtle. He will make a fine breakfast for all of us. We must be careful or he will bite us. Let us throw a net over him and turn him over."

They had no nets with them, so they took some vines, and tore their clothes into strings and made a net.

But when they had put the net all over the Turtle, they could not roll him over. Instead, the Turtle suddenly dived down into the deep water. The men were so eager to get him that they did not let go of the net, so down they went into the water. As they came out they said: "Half the night a Kingfisher kept putting out our fires. Now we have torn

our clothes and got all wet trying to get this Turtle. We will build another fire, and at sunrise we will eat those young Hawks." And they began to build another fire.

The Mother Hawk heard them, and said to her mate: "Sooner or later these men will get our young. Do go and tell our friend the Lion."

At once the Father Hawk flew to the Lion.

"Why do you come at this hour of the night?" asked the Lion.

The Hawk told him the whole story.

The Lion said: "I will come at once. You go back and comfort your mate and the young ones." Soon the Lion came roaring.

When the hunters heard the Lion's roar they cried, "Now we shall all be killed." And away they ran as fast as they could go.

When the Lion came to the foot of the tree, not one of the hunters was to be seen. Then the Kingfisher and the Turtle came up, and the Hawks said: "You have saved us. Friends in need are friends indeed."

XIV

THE BRAVE LITTLE BOWMAN

ONCE upon a time there was a little man with a crooked back who was called the wise little bowman because he used his bow and arrow so very well. This crooked little man said to himself: "If I go to the king and ask him to let me join his army, he's sure to ask what a little man like me is good for. I must find some great big man who will take me as his page, and ask the king to take us." So the little bowman went about the city looking for a big man.

One day he saw a big, strong man digging a ditch. "What makes a fine big man like you do such work?" asked the little man.

"I do this work because I can earn a living in no other way," said the big man.

"Dig no more," said the bowman. "There is in this whole country no such bowman as I am; but no king would let me join his army because I am such a little man. I want you to ask the king to let you join the army. He will take you because you are big and strong. I will do the work that you are given to do, and we will divide the pay. In this way we shall both of us earn a good living. Will you come with me and do as I tell you?" asked the little bowman.

"Yes, I will go with you," said the big man.

So together they set out to go to the king. By and by they came to the gates of the palace, and sent word to the king that a wonderful bowman was there. The king sent for the bowman to come before him. Both the big man and the little man went in and, bowing, stood before the king.

The king looked at the big man and asked, "What brings you here?"

"I want to be in your army," said the big man.

"Who is the little man with you?" asked the king.

"He is my page," said the big man.

"What pay do you want?" asked the king.

"A thousand pieces a month for me and my page, O King," said the big man.

"I will take you and your page," said the king.

So the big man and the little bowman joined the king's army.

56

THE BRAVE LITTLE BOWMAN

Now in those days there was a tiger in the forest who had carried off many people. The king sent for the big man and told him to kill that tiger.

The big man told the little bowman what the king said. They went into the forest together, and soon the little bowman shot the tiger.

The king was glad to be rid of the tiger, and gave the big man rich gifts and praised him.

Another day word came that a buffalo was running up and down a certain road. The king told the big man to go and kill that buffalo. The big man and the little man went to the road, and soon the little man shot the buffalo. When they both went back to the king, he gave a bag of money to the big man.

The king and all the people praised the big man, and so one day the big man said to the little man: "I can get on without you. Do you think there's no bowman but yourself?" Many other harsh and unkind things did he say to the little man.

But a few days later a king from a far country marched upon the city and sent a message to its king saying, "Give up your country, or do battle."

The king at once sent his army. The big man was armed and mounted on a war-elephant. But the little bowman

knew that the big man could not shoot, so he took his bow
and seated himself behind the big man.

Then the war-elephant, at the head of the army, went out
of the city. At the first beat of the drums, the big man

shook with fear. "Hold on tight," said the little bowman.
"If you fall off now, you will be killed. You need not be
afraid; I am here."

But the big man was so afraid that he slipped down off

58

the war-elephant's back, and ran back into the city. He did not stop until he reached his home.

"And now to win!" said the little bowman, as he drove the war-elephant into the fight. The army broke into the camp of the king that came from afar, and drove him back to his own country. Then the little bowman led the army back into the city. The king and all the people called him "the brave little bowman." The king made him the chief of the army, giving him rich gifts.

XV

THE FOOLHARDY WOLF

A LION bounded forth from his lair one day, looking north, west, south, and east. He saw a Buffalo and went to kill him.

The Lion ate all of the Buffalo-meat he wanted, and then went down to the lake for a drink.

As the Lion turned to go toward his den for a nap, he came upon a hungry Wolf.

The Wolf had no chance to get away, so he threw himself at the Lion's feet.

"What do you want?" the Lion asked.

"O Lion, let me be your servant," said the Wolf.

"Very well," said the Lion, "serve me, and you shall have good food to eat."

So saying, the Lion went into his den for his nap.

When he woke up, the Lion said to the Wolf: "Each day you must go to the mountain top, and see whether there are any elephants, or ponies, or buffaloes about. If you see any,

come to me and say: 'Great Lion, come forth in thy might.
Food is in sight.' Then I will kill and eat, and give part
of the meat to you."

So day after day the Wolf climbed to the mountain top,
and seeing a pony, or a buffalo, or an elephant, he went back
to the den, and falling at the Lion's feet he said: "Great
Lion, come forth in thy might. Food is in sight."

Then the Lion would bound forth and kill whichever
beast it was, sharing the meat with the Wolf.

Now this Wolf had never had such fine meat to eat, nor
so much. So as time went on, the Wolf grew bigger and
bigger, and stronger and stronger, until he was really proud
of his great size and strength.

"See how big and strong I am," he said to himself.

"Why am I living day after day on food given me by another? I will kill for my own eating. I'll kill an elephant for myself."

So the Wolf went to the Lion, and said: "I want to eat an elephant of my own killing. Will you let me lie in your corner in the den, while you climb the mountain to look out for an elephant? Then when you see one, you come to the den and say, 'Great Wolf, come forth in thy might. Food is in sight.' Then I will kill the elephant."

Said the Lion: "Wolf, only Lions can kill elephants. The world has never seen a Wolf that could kill an elephant. Give up this notion of yours, and eat what I kill."

But no matter what the Lion said, the Wolf would not give way. So at last the Lion said: "Well, have your own way. Lie down in the den, and I will climb to the top of the mountain."

When he saw an elephant the Lion went back to the mouth of the cave, and said: "Great Wolf, come forth in thy might. Food is in sight."

Then from the den the Wolf nimbly bounded forth, ran to where the elephant was, and, howling three times, he sprang at the elephant.

But the Wolf missed his aim, and fell down at the ele-

phant's feet. The elephant raised his right foot and killed the Wolf.

Seeing all this, the Lion said, "You will no more come forth in your might, you foolhardy Wolf."

XVI

THE STOLEN PLOW

AT one time there were two traders who were great friends. One of them lived in a small village, and one lived in a large town near-by.

One day the village trader took his plow to the large town to have it mended. Then he left it with the trader who lived there. After some time the town trader sold the plow, and kept the money.

When the trader from the village came to get his plow the town trader said, "The mice have eaten your plow."

"That is strange! How could mice eat such a thing?" said the village trader.

That afternoon when all the children went down to the river to go swimming, the village trader took the town trader's little son to the house of a friend saying, "Please keep this little boy here until I come back for him."

By and by the villager went back to the town trader's house.

"Where is my son? He went away with you. Why did n't you bring him back?" asked the town trader.

"I took him with me and left him on the bank of the river while I went down into the water," said the villager. "While I was swimming about a big bird seized your son, and flew up into the air with him. I shouted, but I could not make the bird let go," he said.

"That cannot be true," cried the town trader. "No bird could carry off a boy. I will go to the court, and you will have to go there, and tell the judge."

The villager said, "As you please"; and they both went to the court. The town trader said to the judge:

"This fellow took my son with him to the river, and when I asked where the boy was, he said that a bird had carried him off."

"What have you to say?" said the judge to the village trader.

"I told the father that I took the boy with me, and that a bird had carried him off," said the village trader.

"But where in the world are there birds strong enough to carry off boys?" said the judge.

"I have a question to ask you," answered the village trader. "If birds cannot carry off boys, can mice eat plows?"

"What do you mean by that?" asked the judge.

"I left my good plow with this man. When I came for

it he told me that the mice had eaten it. If mice eat plows, then birds carry off boys; but if mice cannot do this, neither can birds carry off boys. This man says the mice ate my plow."

The judge said to the town trader, "Give back the plow to this man, and he will give your son back to you."

And the two traders went out of the court, and by night-time one had his son back again, and the other had his plow.

XVII

THE LION IN BAD COMPANY

ONE day a young Lion came suddenly upon a Wolf. The Wolf was not able to get away, so he said to the Lion: "Please, Great Lion, could you take me to your den, and let me live with you and your mate? I will work for you all my days."

This young Lion had been told by his father and mother not to make friends with any Wolf. But when this Wolf called him "Great Lion," he said to himself: "This Wolf is not bad. This Wolf is not like other Wolves." So he took the Wolf to the den where he lived with his father and mother.

Now this Lion's father was a fine old Lion, and he told his son that he did not like having this Wolf there. But the young Lion thought he knew better than his father, so the Wolf stayed in the den.

One day the Wolf wanted horse-flesh to eat, so he said to the young Lion, "Sir, there is nothing we have not eaten except horse-meat; let us take a horse."

THE LION IN BAD COMPANY

"But where are there horses?" asked the Lion.

"There are small ponies on the river bank," said the Wolf.

So the young Lion went with the Wolf to the river bank when the ponies were bathing. The Lion caught a small pony, and throwing it on his back, he ran back to his den.

His father said: "My son, those ponies belong to the king. Kings have many skilful archers. Lions do not live long who eat ponies belonging to the king. Do not take another pony."

But the young Lion liked the taste of horse-meat, and he caught and killed pony after pony.

Soon the king heard that a Lion was killing the ponies when they went to bathe in the river. "Build a tank inside the town," said the king. "The lion will not get the ponies there." But the Lion killed the ponies as they bathed in the tank.

Then the king said the ponies must be kept in the stables. But the Lion went over the wall, and killed the ponies in their stables.

At last the king called an archer, who shot like lightning. "Do you think you can shoot this Lion?" the king asked

70

THE LION IN BAD COMPANY

him. The archer said that he was sure he could. "Very well," said the king, "take your place in the tower on the wall, and shoot him." So the archer waited there in the tower.

By and by the Lion and the Wolf came to the wall. The Wolf did not go over the wall but waited to see what would happen. The Lion sprang over the wall. Very soon he caught and killed a pony. Then the archer let fly an arrow.

The Lion roared, "I am shot."

Then the Wolf said to himself: "The Lion has been shot, and soon he will die. I will now go back to my old home in the woods." And so he did.

The Lion fell down dead.

XVIII

THE WISE GOAT AND THE WOLF

ONCE upon a time, many, many wild Goats lived in a cave in the side of a hill. A Wolf lived with his mate not far from this cave. Like all Wolves they liked the taste of Goat-meat. So they caught the Goats, one after another, and ate them all but one who was wiser than all the others. Try as they might, the Wolves could not catch her.

One day the Wolf said to his mate: "My dear, let us play a trick on that wise Goat. I will lie down here pretending to be dead. You go alone to the cave where the Goat lives, and looking very sad, say to her: 'My dear, do you see my mate lying there dead? I am so sad; I have no friends. Will you be good to me? Will you come and help me bury the body of my mate?' The Goat will be sorry for you and I think she will come here with you. When she stands beside me I will spring upon her and bite her in the neck.

72

Then she will fall over dead, and we shall have good meat to eat."

The Wolf then lay down, and his mate went to the Goat, saying what she had been told to say.

But the wise Goat said: "My dear, all my family and friends have been eaten by your mate. I am afraid to go one step with you. I am far safer here than I would be there."

"Do not be afraid," said the Wolf. "What harm can a dead Wolf do to you?"

These and many more words the Wolf said to the Goat, so that at last the Goat said she would go with the Wolf.

But as they went up the hill side by side, the Goat said to herself: "Who knows what will happen? How do I know the Wolf is dead?" She said to the Wolf, "I think it will be better if you go on in front of me."

The Wolf thought he heard them coming. He was hungry and he raised up his head to see if he could see them. The Goat saw him raise his head, and she turned and ran back to her cave.

"Why did you raise your head when you were pretending to be dead?" the Wolf asked her mate. He had no good answer.

By and by the Wolves were both so very hungry that the

Wolf asked his mate to try once more to catch the Goat.

This time the Wolf went to the Goat and said: "My friend, your coming helped us, for as soon as you came, my

mate felt better. He is now very much better. Come and talk to him. Let us be friends and have a good time together."

THE WISE GOAT AND THE WOLF

The wise Goat thought: "These wicked Wolves want to play another trick on me. But I have thought of a trick to play on them." So the Goat said: "I will go to see your mate, and I will take my friends with me. You go back and get ready for us. Let us all have a good time together."

Then the Wolf was afraid, and she asked: "Who are the friends who will come with you? Tell me their names."

The wise Goat said: "I will bring the two Hounds, Old Gray and Young Tan, and that fine big dog called Four-Eyes. And I will ask each of them to bring his mate."

The Wolf waited to hear no more. She turned, and away she ran back to her mate. The Goat never saw either of them again.

XIX

PRINCE WICKED AND THE GRATEFUL ANIMALS

ONCE upon a time a king had a son named Prince Wicked. He was fierce and cruel, and he spoke to nobody without abuse, or blows. Like grit in the eye, was Prince Wicked to every one, both in the palace and out of it.

His people said to one another, "If he acts this way while he is a prince, how will he act when he is king?"

One day when the prince was swimming in the river, suddenly a great storm came on, and it grew very dark.

In the darkness the servants who were with the prince swam from him, saying to themselves, "Let us leave him alone in the river, and he may drown."

When they reached the shore, some of the servants who had not gone into the river said, "Where is Prince Wicked?"

"Is n't he here?" they asked. "Perhaps he came out of the river in the darkness and went home." Then the servants all went back to the palace.

76

The king asked where his son was, and again the servants said: "Isn't he here, O King? A great storm came on soon after we went into the water. It grew very dark. When we came out of the water the prince was not with us."

At once the king had the gates thrown open. He and all his men searched up and down the banks of the river for the missing prince. But no trace of him could be found.

In the darkness the prince had been swept down the river. He was crying for fear he would drown when he came across a log. He climbed upon the log, and floated farther down the river.

When the great storm arose, the water rushed into the homes of a Rat and a Snake who lived on the river bank. The Rat and the Snake swam out into the river and found the same log the prince had found. The Snake climbed upon one end of the log, and the Rat climbed upon the other.

On the river's bank a cottonwood-tree grew, and a young Parrot lived in its branches. The storm pulled up this tree, and it fell into the river. The heavy rain beat down the Parrot when it tried to fly, and it could not go far. Looking down it saw the log and flew down to rest. Now there were four on the log floating down stream together.

Just around the bend in the river a certain poor man had built himself a hut. As he walked to and fro late at night

listening to the storm, he heard the loud cries of the prince.
The poor man said to himself: "I must get that man out
of the water. I must save his life." So he shouted: "I
will save you! I will save you!" as he swam out in the
river.

Soon he reached the log, and pushing it by one end, he

soon pushed it into the bank. The prince jumped up and
down, he was so glad to be safe and sound on dry land.

Then the poor man saw the Snake, the Rat, and the Parrot, and carried them to his hut. He built a fire, putting
the animals near it so they could get dry. He took care of
them first, because they were the weaker, and afterwards
he looked after the comfort of the prince.

Then the poor man brought food and set it before them, looking after the animals first and the prince afterwards. This made the young prince angry, and he said to himself: "This poor man does not treat me like a prince. He takes

care of the animals before taking care of me." Then the prince began to hate the poor man.

A few days later, when the prince, and the Snake, the Rat, and the Parrot were rested, and the storm was all over, the Snake said good-by to the poor man with these words·

79

"Father, you have been very kind to me. I know where there is some buried gold. If ever you want gold, you have only to come to my home and call, 'Snake!' and I will show you the buried gold. It shall all be yours."

Next the Rat said good-by to the poor man. "If ever you want money," said the Rat, "come to my home, and call out, 'Rat!' and I will show you where a great deal of money is buried near my home. It shall all be yours."

Then the Parrot came, saying: "Father, silver and gold have I none, but if you ever want choice rice, come to where I live and call, 'Parrot!' and I will call all my family and friends together, and we will gather the choicest rice in the fields for you."

Last came the prince. In his heart he hated the poor man who had saved his life. But he pretended to be as thankful as the animals had been, saying, "Come to me when I am king, and I will give you great riches." So saying, he went away.

Not long after this the prince's father died, and Prince Wicked was made king. He was then very rich.

By and by the poor man said to himself: "Each of the four whose lives I saved made a promise to me. I will see if they will keep their promises."

PRINCE WICKED AND GRATEFUL ANIMALS

First of all he went to the Snake, and standing near his hole, the poor man called out, "Snake!"

At once the Snake darted forth, and with every mark of respect he said: "Father, in this place there is much gold. Dig it up and take it all."

"Very well," said the poor man. "When I need it, I will not forget."

After visiting for a while, the poor man said good-by to the Snake, and went to where the Rat lived, calling out, "Rat!"

The Rat came at once, and did as the Snake had done, showing the poor man where the money was buried.

"When I need it, I will come for it," said the poor man.

Going next to the Parrot, he called out, "Parrot!" and the bird flew down from the tree-top as soon as he heard the call.

"O Father," said the Parrot, "shall I call together all my family and friends to gather choice rice for you?"

The poor man, seeing that the Parrot was willing and ready to keep his promise, said: "I do not need rice now. If ever I do, I will not forget your offer."

Last of all, the poor man went into the city where the king lived. The king, seated on his great white elephant, was riding through the city. The king saw the poor man, and said to himself: "That poor man has come to ask me for the great riches I promised to give him. I must have his head cut off before he can tell the people how he saved my life when I was the prince."

So the king called his servants to him and said: "You see that poor man over there? Seize him and bind him, beat him at every corner of the street as you march him out of the city, and then chop off his head."

The servants had to obey their king. So they seized and bound the poor man. They beat him at every corner of the street. The poor man did not cry out, but he said, over and over again, "It is better to save poor, weak animals than to save a prince."

At last some wise men among the crowds along the street asked the poor man what prince he had saved. Then the poor man told the whole story, ending with the words, "By saving your king, I brought all this pain upon myself."

The wise men and all the rest of the crowd cried out: "This poor man saved the life of our king, and now the king has ordered him to be killed. How can we be sure that he will not have any, or all, of us killed? Let us kill him." And in their anger they rushed from every side upon the king as he rode on his elephant, and with arrows and stones they killed him then and there.

Then they made the poor man king, and set him to rule over them.

The poor man ruled his people well. One day he decided once more to try the Snake, the Rat, and the Parrot. So, followed by many servants, the king went to where the Snake lived.

At the call of "Snake!" out came the Snake from his hole, saying, "Here, O King, is your treasure; take it."

"I will," said the king. "And I want you to come with me."

Then the king had his servants dig up the gold.

Going to where the Rat lived, the king called, "Rat!" Out came the Rat, and bowing low to the king, the Rat said, "Take all the money buried here and have your servants carry it away."

"I will," said the king, and he asked the Rat to go with him and the Snake.

Then the king went to where the Parrot lived, and called, "Parrot!" The Parrot flew down to the king's feet and said, "O King, shall I and my family and my friends gather choice rice for you?"

"Not now, not until rice is needed," said the king. "Will you come with us?" The Parrot was glad to join them.

So with the gold, and the money, and with the Snake, the Rat, and the Parrot as well, the king went back to the city.

The king had the gold and the money hidden away in the palace. He had a tube of gold made for the Snake to live in. He had a glass box made for the Rat's home, and a cage of gold for the Parrot. Each had the food he liked best of all to eat every day, and so these four lived happily all their lives.

CHINESE WICKED AND GRATEFUL ANIMALS

XX

BEAUTY AND BROWNIE

TWO Deer named Beauty and Brownie lived with their father and mother and great herds of Deer in a forest. One day their father called them to him and said: "The Deer in the forest are always in danger when the corn is ripening in the fields. It will be best for you to go away for a while, and you must each take your own herd of Deer with you."

"What is the danger, Father?" they asked.

"When the Deer go into the fields to eat the corn they get caught in the traps the men set there," the father said. "Many Deer are caught in these traps every year."

"Shall you go away with us?" Brownie said.

"No, your mother and I, and some of the other old Deer will stay here in the forest," said the father. "There will be food enough for us, but there is not enough for you and your herds. You must lead your herds up into the high hills where there is plenty of food for you, and stay there

until the crops are all cut. Then you can bring your herds
back here. But you must be careful.

"You must travel by night, because the hunters will see
you if you go by day. And you must not take your herd
near the villages where hunters live."

So Beauty and Brownie and their herds set out. Beauty
traveled at night and did not go near any villages, and at
last brought his herd safely to the high hills. Not a single
Deer did Beauty lose.

But Brownie forgot what his father had said. Early each
morning he started off with his herd, going along all through
the day. When he saw a village, he led his herd right past

it. Again and again hunters saw the herd, and they killed many, many of the Deer in Brownie's herd.

When crops had been cut, the Deer started back to the forest. Beauty led all his herd back, but stupid Brownie traveled in the daytime, and again he took his herd past the villages. When he reached the forest only a few were left of all Brownie's herd.

XXI

THE ELEPHANT AND THE DOG

ONCE upon a time a Dog used to go into the stable where the king's Elephant lived. At first the Dog went there to get the food that was left after the Elephant had finished eating.

Day after day the Dog went to the stable, waiting around for bits to eat. But by and by the Elephant and the Dog came to be great friends. Then the Elephant began to share his food with the Dog, and they ate together. When the Elephant slept, his friend the Dog slept beside him. When the Elephant felt like playing, he would catch the Dog in his trunk and swing him to and fro. Neither the Dog nor the Elephant was quite happy unless the other was near-by.

One day a farmer saw the Dog and said to the Elephant-keeper: "I will buy that Dog. He looks good-tempered, and I see that he is smart. How much do you want for the Dog?"

THE ELEPHANT AND THE DOG

The Elephant-keeper did not care for the Dog, and he did want some money just then. So he asked a fair price, and the farmer paid it and took the Dog away to the country.

The king's Elephant missed the Dog and did not care to eat when his friend was not there to share the food. When the time came for the Elephant to bathe, he would not bathe. The next day again the Elephant would not eat, and he would not bathe. The third day, when the Elephant would neither eat nor bathe, the king was told about it.

The king sent for his chief servant, saying, "Go to the stable and find out why the Elephant is acting in this way."

The chief servant went to the stable and looked the Elephant all over. Then he said to the Elephant-keeper: "There seems to be nothing the matter with this Elephant's body, but why does he look so sad? Has he lost a play-mate?"

"Yes," said the keeper, "there was a Dog who ate and

THE ELEPHANT AND THE DOG

slept and played with the Elephant. The Dog went away three days ago."

"Do you know where the Dog is now?" asked the chief servant.

"No, I do not," said the keeper.

Then the chief servant went back to the king and said.

"The Elephant is not sick, but he is lonely without his friend, the Dog."

"Where is the Dog?" asked the king.

"A farmer took him away, so the Elephant-keeper says," said the chief servant. "No one knows where the farmer lives."

"Very well," said the king. "I will send word all over the country, asking the man who bought this Dog to turn him loose. I will give him back as much as he paid for the Dog."

When the farmer who had bought the Dog heard this, he turned him loose. The Dog ran back as fast as ever he could go to the Elephant's stable. The Elephant was so glad to see the Dog that he picked him up with his trunk and put him on his head. Then he put him down again.

When the Elephant-keeper brought food, the Elephant watched the Dog as he ate, and then took his own food.

All the rest of their lives the Elephant and the Dog lived together.